Chasing EMBER

ARIELLA MONTI

sweet
magnolia
media

1st edition 2025
eBook ISBN 979-8-9920601-8-8
Print ISBN 979-8-9920601-7-1

Cover Design Disturbed Valkyrie Design
Editing Owl Eyes Proofs and Edits

Adult – Contemporary Romance – Standalone novella

Dedication

To North Carolina.

The imperfect place that became my perfect

home.

Before we begin

Content Advisory

Chasing Ember is a cozy, low-stakes romance with a happy ending. But please be aware that this novella is intended for readers 18 years and older and includes:

Explicit descriptions of sexual intimacy
Explicit language
References to nonconsensual power imbalances in intimate relationships

To Appalachia with Love

Chasing Ember was originally published as a short story in To Appalachia with Love: A Charity Romance Anthology in November 2024. The anthology project organized by NC Indies: North Carolina Indie Authors raised more than $5,000 benefiting nonprofit organizations in western North Carolina following Hurricane Helene.

I always intended on expanding *Chasing Ember* into a full novella and I'm thrilled to give you 10,000 more words of Jack and Mia (AKA Siena in the anthology version).

If you'd like to read the original short story, you can get it free by joining my mailing list, or you can still get the full anthology by visiting ncindieauthors.com/wnc-charity-anthology

Mia

"June! No!" Mia Chase struggled to watch her step and her sandy yellow lab as they both ran down the narrow switchback trail. Dragging her purple leash behind her, June wasn't concerned with the exposed roots and rocks that made for easily sprained human ankles.

It was one of the first crisp Appalachian mornings after a brutal summer, and this was supposed to be a nice relaxing hike to get Mia's mind off all the work stuff waiting for her back in town. But she made the mistake of pulling out her phone while June sniffed a popular pee-tree halfway around the familiar Mossy Creek Loop.

It was during her distracted scrolling that a notification from her—former—internet provider popped up demanding payment for services rendered or cease to connect to the World Wide Web. In the few seconds it took for Mia to think, *but I canceled that*, Juniper Kimberly Chase (her government name) took off at full speed, pulling the leash out of Mia's loose grip.

Needless to say, this impromptu trail run in the wrong bra was neither nice nor relaxing.

June rounded a corner and splashed through a stream when another hiker came into view.

"Fuuuuuuuuck," Mia groaned. June wasn't an aggressive dog, but she also wasn't the type to take off.

"June! Stop!" Mia yelled fruitlessly.

While her canine ignored her, the hiker kneeled and kept his hands low and loose. It's not at all how Mia would have reacted to a loose dog, but it worked. June's gait changed from a run to an excited dance right into the man's arms. Approaching a stranger like they were long-lost best friends was definitely better than the bloodbath Mia's anxiety envisioned.

The stranger slid his hand through the top of the leash and spoiled June with the kind of affection Mia didn't think the dog deserved at the moment.

"Thank you so much!" Mia panted. She took the leash from his outstretched hand and looped it around her wrist as she breathed through the stitch forming in her side.

The stranger laughed, his wide smile the only thing visible from under the brim of his App State ball cap.

"I knew there was a reason I skipped leg day at the gym."

Mia glanced at his legs. He wore mesh basketball shorts that exposed thick thighs, muscular calves, and tattoos that snaked around his limbs and disappeared under his clothes.

He scratched behind June's ears once more before standing to his full height. The earthy green in his hazel eyes perfectly complemented his hickory-brown beard salted with white. It was a striking combination, but it was his mouth that Mia was most drawn to; full lips of the darkest pink that rested in a mischievous smile.

Once her brain pieced his features together, Mia's breath hitched with recognition, and she prayed he didn't notice. The lips, the eyes, and the meaty legs belonged to singer, songwriter, and occasional Broadway actor, Jackson Hunter.

Mia didn't regularly follow celebrity news, but she was enough of a fan of his music that she'd heard he recently divorced the Hollywood actor he once called his muse and moved out of their shared Los Angeles mansion. The state visitors bureau wouldn't let anyone forget he was a North Carolina native. Still, she hadn't expected to find him here in Firefly Ridge.

"Which gym do you go to?" she asked, then wished she could take it back. For mere mortals, it was a perfectly reasonable follow-up question, but Jackson Hunter was anything but mere, and he probably wanted to keep his workout spot quiet.

He surprised her by answering. "Champion Fitness over on Maple Avenue. Do you know it?"

"I do." She nodded. "I own the yoga studio around the block on Cypress."

"People have been trying to get me into yoga forever," he said, a hint of embarrassment in his voice. "It never stuck."

"Maybe you haven't had the right teacher."

Mia didn't have a chance to reflect on how suggestive that sounded. Bored of their conversation, June pulled on the lead to sniff a nearby boulder. The unexpected jolt threw Mia off-balance and into the arms of Grammy winner Jackson Hunter. He held both of her arms to steady her, and she took a few steps to recover.

"Is this how your dog...June? Got away from you?" He let go, his hands hovering close in preparation for another fall.

Mia's body flushed, less from embarrassment and more from the sensation his calloused hands left on her skin. She laughed harder than his joke warranted, but the entire interaction left her off-kilter.

"Juniper. June for short. And yes, pretty much." Mia sighed. "Anyway, beginners are kind of my specialty, in case you ever want to give yoga another try."

June tugged on the lead again, and Mia narrowed her eyes at her beloved dog, who had zero appreciation for the man they were speaking to.

"You better get moving before she drags you out of here," he said, squatting to rub June's ears and accept a few more sloppy licks.

"You're probably right. My health insurance sucks, and I can't afford a broken ankle. Thanks for grabbing her, Jackson."

Fuck. Fuck. Fuck.

They never exchanged names. The horror smothered her like an avalanche. Mia wanted to crumble into dust and blow away on the mountain breeze.

"Sure thing," Jackson said, his voice softer now. He seemed to hesitate, unsure what to say or do next.

"I should g—"

"Give me your number," he interrupted and pulled his phone from his pocket. "To your studio. Or at least the name. So I can take a yoga class."

"Oh! Yeah! Totally." Flustered and poorly hiding it, Mia took the phone and messaged herself with shaky fingers. While doing so, she wondered what portal she walked through to end up in a universe where she was giving her number to Jackson Hunter.

"I'm Mia, by the way."

"Jackson. But you already knew that." He winked. "I prefer Jack, though."

Mia laughed and looked down at her feet. Then anywhere else that wasn't the devilish grin plastered on his gorgeous face.

"Well, Jack," Mia said, emphasizing his name with a hard K. "I'm gonna go before I make an even bigger ass out of myself."

"Be good for your mom, Junie," Jack said with one last scratch behind the dog's ear.

Mia said goodbye and let June lead them back down the trail. Smiling to herself, Mia looked over her shoulder and caught Jack still watching her. He put one hand in his pocket and raised the other in an awkward wave before turning around to head in the opposite direction.

Well, at least now they were even.

Jack

Dawn teased the eastern sky over the modest cabin in North Carolina's Blue Ridge Mountains. After another restless night, Jack had given up on his dreams of sleeping late and shuffled into the kitchen.

The cabin was quiet except for the coffee's steady drip into the carafe and the taunting of his guitar propped against the couch. It dared him to strum a few chords, but Jack couldn't make his legs move. It was too early in the morning for the kind of frustration and disappointment that accompanied him whenever he tried to play.

He ended his staring contest with the acoustic instrument when he heard the sputtered popping of the coffee maker, its primitive signal that the pot was full and ready to be emptied.

Jack pulled his worn college hoodie over his bare chest and stepped out onto the second-floor deck, taking care not to slam the door behind him.

Not that it would matter; he was there alone. That was the point of this whole thing. *The thing* being renting out Richie's family's cabin for a few months so he could detox from whatever it was that kept him from writing.

Jack eased himself back into an Adirondack chair and set his coffee on the table beside him. A few bats fluttered across the indigo sky, getting their last bite for the night.

Jack scratched the thick paint on the arm. He wondered how many coats it took Richie's dad to cover the vulgarities Jack and his high school buddies carved into the wood twenty-some-odd years ago.

When they weren't destroying Richie's parents' outdoor furniture, they were writing angsty rock music. They played for hours into the night, living on cold pizza and chasing it with warm beer. In a smoky haze, Jack, Richie, and the two other guys that made up Concrete Tears, channeled their adolescent, middle-class, white-boy emotions into music inspired by Nirvana, Smashing Pumpkins, and Green Day.

The memories were fuzzy, covered by the paint of age (and a lot of weed). But like the fresh air, the emotions engulfed him the moment he parked in the familiar gravel driveway. He arrived there full of optimism, but whatever magic the Blue Ridge cabin held two decades ago failed to materialize, and the pages of Jack's brand-new notebook remained empty.

He fished through the deep pockets of his flannel lounge pants for his phone. The first day he woke up before the sun it felt like blasphemy to ruin a perfectly tranquil morning with technology. But three weeks later, sleeping past dawn continued to elude him, and he no longer cared.

But for the first time in three weeks, he skipped all his social media apps and went straight to his messages where he found Mia's text from his phone to herself.

JACK: This guy gets a week's worth of free yoga passes for catching your terrible dog. Mia Chase, Chasing Ember Yoga Studio.

Jack lost count of how many times he read it and how many times it made him laugh.

He'd heard Mia's yells echoing through the forest a few minutes before seeing her dog bounding through a stream and towards him at full speed. In hindsight, putting himself in front of a strange runaway dog wasn't his smartest idea, but he didn't regret it. The puppy love he got from Juniper eased the dour mood he began his hike with, and anything left vanished once he laid eyes on the dog's owner.

Mia Chase was a gorgeous mess. Her lightly freckled skin was flushed cardinal red, and small beads of sweat trailed from her collarbone and disappeared under the neck of her flowy crop top. Her chest heaved as she caught her breath, the movements lifting her shirt just enough to flash a sliver of a tattoo on her torso. Some of her dark purple hair had escaped its braid and fell haphazardly around her glistening face.

He didn't usually equate a hard workout with bedroom activities and instantly felt like a creep for envisioning Mia in that way before learning her name. Then again, he'd had little interest in sex the past year, so maybe his explicit thoughts were a sign of a healing broken heart.

Jack quickly scrolled through Chasing Ember's social media pages, slowing for any post with Mia in the picture. The frequency dwindled after a few dozen posts, around the same time there was a drastic change in the content's vibe. Some of the older images made his stomach churn: shallow affirmations and good-vibes-only messaging. Pitches for questionable supplements and expensive yoga retreats promising a life-altering spiritual adventure.

He chewed on this newfound intel as the rising sun turned the ancient Appalachians into a silhouette against a fiery pink and orange sky. Mia didn't strike him as someone who dabbled in toxic wellness, but he'd been wrong before. The more recent posts looked pretty balanced; one slide extolled the health benefits of some plant called yarrow, while another advertised an upcoming flu shot clinic at the local library. There was a link for a playlist of free guided meditations on the studio website and memes that didn't even try to hide her political leanings. The About section on every platform mentioned the studio being a queer-owned business complete with an emoji of the bisexual pride flag. Jack being pansexual likely wouldn't faze her, and that brought him more relief than expected.

He came to the cabin in Firefly Ridge to avoid distractions, and Mia Chase was turning into a tempting distraction.

Mia

The satisfaction of slamming a receiver onto its base was one of the few reasons Mia still had a desktop office phone at the studio. After an hour on hold with her former internet provider, she channeled all her frustration into hanging up as aggressively as possible without breaking the stupid thing.

She barely took a complete breath when a new email from the power company appeared on her screen.

"Now fucking what?" she mumbled, clicking on the message.

Mia stared at the unpaid bill long enough to dry her contact lenses and blur her vision. The total was now more than double because it covered two billing periods plus late fees. She could've sworn she had put it on autopay a few months earlier after her [former] business partner, Ember, sold Mia her share of the studio and the building that housed it.

In Mia's opinion, Ember was a mediocre yoga teacher, but it was an undeniable fact that the other woman was much better at operating a business. Ember handled the finances, like paying the electric bill, because Mia, in her own words, "fucking sucked at it."

Mia also had a second job at the local community college teaching yoga for physical education credits. Taking over the entirety of the business during summer break led Mia to severely overestimate her ability to juggle both.

The unpaid electric bill with the warning that lack of payment would result in a stoppage of service only seemed to prove Mia's point. At that moment, she was having a hard time accessing the radical acceptance necessary to show herself some compassion.

Fighting the urge to put it off until after her class, Mia paid the bill and set up autopay. The studio was doing well—better even—after Ember's departure, so she had the money to cover the extra fees. But with winter weather and a predictably slower season only a couple of months away, Mia didn't want to burn any extra profit on interest and late fees.

The printer was churning out the autopay confirmation when the soft bells over the door chimed, announcing the arrival of a tall, floppy-haired distraction.

"Hey." Without his ball cap hiding his face from the natural light, the saturated greens and copper browns of Jack's eyes popped against his dark, graying hair and light skin.

"You made it." Her voice squeaked with surprise. Mia hadn't actually expected Jack to step foot in her studio. Though tempted, she didn't even bother saving his number because she assumed they'd never speak again. And yet, there he stood looking at her with those damned captivating eyes and roguish smile.

"I tried registering online, but the service is really spotty where I'm staying." He looked a little embarrassed at the admission. "And I don't have a mat or anything."

"No worries." Mia pulled up a blank registration form on her tablet and handed it to Jack. "I have everything you need."

That devilish smile returned. "I thought you would."

Mia's stomach twisted, and she chewed on her lip in a terrible attempt to hide her smile. She needed to busy herself with something, but there was nothing to fidget with, so she just stood there basking in Jackson Hunter's everything while struggling to keep her thoughts professional.

He was dressed much the same way as the day before: gold and black basketball shorts and a white athletic shirt that stretched across his chest and shoulders. The sporty look was a stark contrast to his musician aesthetic, which involved a lot more leather, dark-wash denim, and silver jewelry. He looked less like a rock star and more like one of the college boys who played disc golf at the course down the road.

Jack handed her the tablet, and she reviewed it quickly before giving him a visual tour of the space, pointing out where he could leave his things, what props to grab, and where to find them.

"You can't exactly get lost in here," Mia joked.

"It's really cozy," Jack replied. "It feels welcoming."

Mia put her hand on her chest, and her eyes widened in appreciation. "Thank you for saying that. I've been redecorating, and that's what I was hoping for."

Before selling the building to Mia, Ember had final say over its decor and layout. It wasn't that the previous design wasn't welcoming; it was just that it seemed more welcoming to a specific clientele than to others.

Now that it was hers, Mia could do whatever she wanted, and a makeover was one of the first things to happen.

Her regulars started to trickle in, prompting Mia to finish her studio introduction.

"Remind me," she said. "What's your experience with yoga?"

Jack laughed through his nose. "My ex was really into it, so I went with him when we were both in town at the same time. But I didn't like it enough to keep at it when we were apart."

Mia nodded, filing away the subtext she caught. "In my experience, that's pretty common with couples, believe it or not. Is there anything going on with your body that you think I should be aware of?"

Again with the devilish smile.

But this time, it was accompanied by flushed cheeks and an averted gaze.

"Like injuries, surgeries, chronic illnesses," Mia added.

'Right." He exhaled a laugh. "I got diagnosed with carpal tunnel not too long ago. But uhh, I haven't been playing much so it hasn't really been bothering me."

Mia nodded as she mentally put together a few more pieces of this puzzle. "As I cue each posture, I'll go over how you can manage or alleviate any wrist pain, but if something hurts in a bad way, stop doing it. We don't do pain here."

"My fitness trainer doesn't share the same philosophy." Jack chuckled.

"Pain's not always a bad thing."

Though he didn't say a word, Jack's face replied loudly.

"What I mean is," Mia rushed to clarify, "if there's a sensation that feels good, lean into it. If it doesn't, don't do it."

It was the same spiel she said to every new student and at the beginning of every class, but something about Jack Hunter made everything she said sound especially sexual.

"Last thing," she said and handed him a coaster-sized card. "This is for hands-on assists. One side tells me you welcome them, the other tells me you don't. I always ask before touching someone, but this gives me a heads-up for how to approach a student."

Jack turned the card over a few times like he'd never seen anything like it before. "Cool."

"You can go get set up, and I'll be in soon," Mia encouraged.

Still looking a bit nervous, Jack disappeared into the practice space.

Mia took a deep breath and exhaled slowly. Maybe Jack Hunter was going to be too much of a distraction.

Jack

Jack set up his mat in the back corner of the small room. Normally, he wouldn't box himself in, but it was near a nook piled high with cushions and pillows, and he was drawn in by the coziness.

Everything about the studio was cozy. Natural sunlight from high windows poured into the space, diffused by sheer curtains. Thriving houseplants sat in every corner. The furniture in the seating area was slightly mismatched as though Mia was looking for function and comfort over aesthetics. A small bookcase behind him was packed tightly with a variety of books. He squinted at the spines and regretted leaving his new glasses in the car.

The room had filled since he had set up his mat. Jack counted nine students, including himself, most speaking with each other in hushed tones. Being over forty, Jack was used to being one of the oldest in a room filled with people barely old enough to buy alcohol. But in a surprise turn, more than half the attendees looked to be older than him. The youngest appeared to be in her early twenties, and she sat in a chair next to a thick, bright pink mat. A cane adorned with stickers lay across her lap.

If they noticed him, or recognized him, they were doing a great job pretending they were unimpressed by his presence. When he was younger, the apathy would have bruised his ego, but now he preferred going unnoticed.

When she walked into the room, Mia Chase didn't go unnoticed. The chatter died down as she closed the curtain that separated the reception area from the practice space. She had a subtle way of commanding attention. Less like an authority figure and more like the cool high school art teacher that genuinely loved every mediocre piece her students created.

The sheer sides of her dark gray leggings ran from her calves to her mid-thigh. He was sure he could see one partially exposed tattoo, but he couldn't be sure without those damn glasses. Her billowy tank top flowed over her soft hips and stomach and showed off more tattoos on her toned arms and shoulders. She'd tied her purple-colored hair up in a ponytail and pinned her long bangs away from her face. One of her students made her laugh, and Jack found himself unwittingly envious of the person who elicited Mia's beaming smile.

Mia sat cross-legged on her own mat and ran through what sounded like a typical welcome. Her voice was casual and friendly and not at all like the soothing whispers he'd heard from other teachers.

"Let's get started." She locked eyes with Jack and gave him an encouraging smile that made his heart pound and his hands sweat.

Guided by Mia's voice, Jack closed his eyes and took a few long breaths. He fidgeted a bit, adjusting to the discomfort of intentional stillness. He was hyperaware of his racing heartbeat that refused to slow. Another exhale, and he noticed his teeth were clenched.

He wondered how long they'd been like that.

He relaxed his jaw and his forehead with it.

He wasn't quite relaxed when Mia began a warm-up flow. Despite his inexperience, Jack followed her cues with ease. She offered alternatives and suggested prop usage without judgment and confidently used them herself.

"I invite you to come to warrior two, bending your front knee into a lunge as deep as you're feeling today," Mia instructed. "I chased my dog through the woods yesterday, so I'm not getting low today."

Jack's laugh overpowered the giggles from the rest of the class. He almost lost his balance, but recovered just as Mia added, "But maybe you want to make up for skipping leg day. Whatever."

Harder laughs and a few groans broke out. Jack caught Mia's gaze and lowered his lunge until he felt a satisfying burn in his thigh. She flashed him a smile before stepping off her mat to assist another student.

Completely focused on his body's movements, Jack was able to get out of his head for the first time in weeks. Easing into the end of class, Mia dimmed the lights and helped a few students get settled into comfortable positions on the floor or in chairs. Following their lead, Jack stuck a bolster under his knees and a blanket under his head. In the quiet, his breath slowed, and his heart rate finally settled into a steady rhythm.

Mia spoke in a voice so soft he could barely hear her over the music. "I'll be coming around to offer a final, gentle hands-on assist. I invite you to flip your card at any point should you change your mind."

Jack opened his eyes and checked his card. A bright green *Yes* was still facing up. His ears followed Mia padding around the room. He tried to ignore her whispers, but he couldn't bring himself to sever that connection.

Hearing the swish of her hands rubbing together, his once steady heartbeat picked up speed in anticipation.

"Jack, I'm behind you," she whispered. "Can I touch you?"

"Yes." He sighed, but it did little to soothe his racing heart.

Mia inhaled long and deep and rubbed her hands together again. She exhaled and gently pressed his shoulders towards the ground, heat radiating from her palms.

The tender pressure released a plug in his body, and the last of his tension drained away. His chest ached when her hands disappeared, but he began to slip into a warm, comfortable place. He wanted to stay in that dreamlike state in the warmth of Mia's touch. But after a length of time completely unknown to him, Mia led them back to the real world.

Again seated on her own mat, Mia thanked her students for attending class and gave everyone a bit of space as they packed up. The energy and the volume increased as they finished catching up with each other. Everyone seemed as relaxed and happy as he felt.

Sitting on a long bench in the lobby, Jack was tying his sneakers when Mia sat down, her body angled toward him.

"So?"

"I definitely need more of this in my life." He was talking about yoga, but the same could be said for having Mia so close. Especially if it would give him the opportunity to make her blush and grin whenever he wanted.

She looked down at her feet. Her toenails were covered in glittery nail stickers. "I'm really happy to hear that."

"I'm happy it makes you happy," he replied, his tone more flirty than intended. She'd looked so sad when he walked in before class, and now the worry in her features was gone.

The chimes over the door rang, and a familiar face stepped through the door. Despite nearly two decades since he'd last seen her, Jack would know Miss Sheila anywhere. Sheila Wiley owned Trixy's Tavern, and she always bent the rules for underage amateur musicians wanting to play on slow nights.

The woman gasped and put a hand on her chest. Her ruby-red lips formed an O, and her thick, mascaraed lashes fluttered. "I was hearing rumors that Jack Hunter was in town," she said. "And here you are."

Jack stood up to hug her. She felt smaller than he remembered, but she also no longer smelled like cigarettes and skunked beer. "The rumors are true."

"Wait, Miss Sheila, how do you know Jack?" Mia asked.

Sheila lifted a hand, encouraging Jack to take the lead.

"In high school, I was in a garage band with a few of my friends."

Sheila jumped in. "Named?"

Jack huffed a laugh. "Concrete Tears."

Mia cackled. "I'm sorry. Please continue." She covered her mouth to suppress her laughter.

"A few times a year, we'd come out to my friend's cabin to write and play music. After we all turned eighteen, Miss Sheila used to let us play gigs at Trixy's. I don't talk about this publicly for obvious reasons."

"I'd let them play on the quiet nights during the week," Sheila added.

"We brought in a decent crowd though." Jack smiled at the memory. "We were out here often enough that the locals knew us even though we lived in Durham. Then Richie and I went to App State and kept playing gigs in the area."

"It helped that Richie's parents lived in that cabin for about a decade before they headed towards Raleigh," Sheila said. "Back then, Richie's dad, Charlie, was one of our best bartenders."

Jack gaped at her. "I don't think I knew that. Is that why you let us in when we were underage?"

The old woman's laugh was more raspy than Jack remembered, but the cadence was the same. It was all the confirmation he needed.

"Miss Sheila, I'll cut your session price in half if you give me more of this Jackson Hunter lore," Mia said with a wink.

"Oh, I've got plenty. We could write a book." She patted Jack's shoulder. "It was good seeing you. I hope we'll be running into each other here more often."

Sheila slipped off her sandals and disappeared into the practice area.

"Sorry for keeping you. I didn't realize you had another class." Jack pulled his keys out of his pocket and took his phone off silent.

"Oh, you're fine." Mia stood up and took a sip from her water bottle. "Miss Sheila does private sessions with me, and I give her a thirty-minute arrival window because her transportation can be a little inconsistent."

Jack knew that was his cue to exit, but he wasn't quite ready to return to a very loud and overstimulating world.

"So will I see you tomorrow?" Mia asked. Hopefulness hinted in her voice.

Clearly being forced to leave, Jack opened the door. "Oh yeah. I'm not letting my dog-catching reward go to waste."

He said goodbye and stepped out into the late morning sunlight, a bit more accepting of all the noise and potential distractions.

Mia

Typical of fall in North Carolina, summer made a brief return, and it was the final straw for the yoga studio's HVAC system. The repair tech diagnosed the problem as something, *"that could have been prevented with regular seasonal maintenance,"* and left her with an estimate for the repair.

In the meantime, several fans worked to keep the space comfortable. Mia wouldn't be the only heat-sensitive person in the building that day, but she'd be the only one that couldn't escape after an hour, and it was already making her cranky.

Mia thought she knew all the risks of getting involved in owning the eighty-five-year-old building; she'd spent nearly every day there over the last five years. As the building's owner, Ember handled the maintenance, and Mia was under the impression that what needed to get done was getting done. Evidently it wasn't, and now Mia was literally paying the consequences.

She took out her irritation on a cardboard box secured with an unreasonable amount of packing tape. She stabbed the top of the box with the blade of her utility knife, tearing open the flaps. The t-shirts inside were thankfully undamaged. The merchandise wasn't even on display yet, and she already had to increase the retail price by a couple of dollars to help cover the looming HVAC bill.

The bells over the door chimed, and Mia's cranky mood dissipated when Jack walked in. The heaviness in her chest, like she was fighting back tears, turned into a stomach flutter.

"It's warm in here today," he observed as he sat down on the bench to untie his sneakers.

"The AC's busted," Mia said. "Protesting another week of summer, I guess."

"The predictable and consistent weather is one of the few things I miss about living in L.A."

Mia couldn't argue with that. North Carolina had approximately fifteen seasons, and they weren't always in the same order. They were currently experiencing what was colloquially known as *Second Summer*.

"Well, I have plenty of shirts for sale if anyone needs a replacement after class." She folded one into a tight rectangle and placed it in a basket.

Jack stood up and walked over. "Can I see?"

Mia handed him a dark green one from the open box.

Jack unfolded it and admired the design. Line-drawn mountains blended seamlessly into a copse of pine trees and flowed into ocean waves. "This is amazing," he said.

"Thank you!" Mia exclaimed. "I drew the design and got them screen printed locally. I'm pretty proud of how they turned out."

"I didn't know you were an artist." Jack took the shirt with him and stepped into the bathroom at the opposite end of the reception area.

"It's just a hobby nowadays," Mia said a little louder so he could hear her behind the door. "It was more of a side hustle before Ember and I opened the studio."

Jack emerged from the bathroom. The shirt was a size too small as evidenced by the way her design stretched across his chest and clung to every muscle and curve. The color was perfect on him, though. It matched the pine green of his hazel eyes and brought out the hint of maple in his dark curls. It even tempered the gray in his beard, turning it to a soft mushroom white instead of snow.

"I like the color," he said. "But I have compression shirts looser than this. I think a large would be more comfortable."

"Right." Mia's breathy reply sounded more seductive than intended.

She grudgingly pulled her gaze away from Jack to dig through the box of green shirts in search of a bigger size.

"Here we go." Mia tugged a shirt free and turned around, finding herself within arm's reach of Jack's bare chest.

Bare wasn't the right word; unclothed was more accurate.

His upper body was a canvas for vibrant tattoos. It was a hodgepodge of color and style depicting a lifetime's worth of sessions with different artists and evolving taste.

And his nipples were pierced.

Did she know his nipples were pierced?

Jack had the physique of someone who had a regular gym routine paired with the softness that came with middle age. A broad, sculpted chest melted into a rounded tummy that hung slightly over the waistband of his shorts.

Mia took the smaller shirt from him and held out the new one. Jack seemed to hesitate as though he also wanted to avoid completing the exchange.

"Oh goodness, sweet baby Jesus!" cried a woman's voice, snapping them both out of the trance they shared.

Jack grabbed the shirt from Mia and apologized profusely while pulling the new, better-fitting shirt over his head.

"Jackson, honey, a lady my age needs a warning before a handsome man takes off his clothes," Sheila Wiley said as she fanned herself with her hand.

Mia was already laughing through Jack's apologies to Sheila and the sweet baby Jesus, and now her eyes were blurring with tears.

While Mia tried desperately to compose herself, Sheila told Jack about a charity concert she was hosting at Trixy's the weekend before Christmas.

"I know if you made an appearance, tickets would go real quick," Sheila said. "Especially if you treat us to some new music."

Trixy's hosted two fundraisers every year, and it was the only time there was a cover charge. The December event, always held on the eve of the winter solstice, raised money for a foundation based in Boone that provided grants for environmental projects across the state.

Jack's posture changed after the request. His shoulders hunched forward, and he ran his hand through his hair a few times, separating the curls.

"Umm, sure," he said. "I have to check my calendar with my manager, but I'll do it."

Jack straightened a bit in response to Sheila's broad smile.

"What's wrong?" Mia asked when the older woman was safely in the practice room.

"I don't have any new music." He lowered his voice to an almost-whisper. "I owe my record label another album, and I have a few open songwriting contracts, but I have nothing. Not one lyric or melody or chord. That's the whole reason I'm back in Firefly Ridge."

Mia nodded and offered him an empathetic smile. "Sometimes deadlines help," she offered. "Or doing something different. Like using a different part of your brain."

"Like what?"

Mia shrugged. "I dunno. Wanna do my bookkeeping?"

"Yes," he answered firmly.

"What?" Now Mia was confused.

"No. I was just joking. And rock stars are notoriously bad with money," she teased. She actually had no idea what Jack's financial situation was.

"I'm not," he said firmly. "Joking, I mean. Or bad with money. Though, it's a valid assumption. I majored in business at App State, and I couldn't always afford an accountant."

Mia's cheeks heated with embarrassment. She bit her nail, considering his offer.

"I can't afford to pay you."

"Good, because I don't want your money."

She really needed a business manager, but even having someone stay on top of her finances could probably prevent at least one of her weekly shame spirals.

"Okay. We'll start after class."

Jack

The way Mia talked about her studio finances, Jack was expecting a marble notebook and a shoebox overflowing with receipts. It wasn't that bad, but Jack understood why Mia had trouble keeping track of everything. Whoever set it up used a collection of spreadsheets formatted in a way that likely made sense only to their creator. The blocks of tiny letters and numbers on Mia's laptop screen made his eyes cross and gave him a headache.

He spent a week researching new bookkeeping software and free tools to keep her accounts current. Another week getting Mia's feedback, and finally a third setting it up.

When he wasn't doing that, he was taking classes at Chasing Ember, hiking the trails along the Blue Ridge Parkway, and completely ignoring his own music-business responsibilities.

He was feeling a little less guilty about that last one lately. Especially when he got to hang out with Mia after class. The days she brought Juniper to work were guilt-free.

Tucked in the cozy corner, Jack had erected a makeshift workstation using a tower of blocks and several bolsters, all so June wouldn't be forced to move from her spot sprawled across his legs. It wasn't exactly comfortable, but it was comforting. A late-season thunderstorm was rolling over Firefly Ridge, and a steady rain pattered against the windows and trickled down the gutters.

The soothing ambient music played during classes was gone, replaced by a playlist that sounded like the mix CD that he still occasionally listened to in his car.

Every few tracks he'd call out, "Good song!" and Mia would stop cleaning to share a memory she associated with it.

The one from the first album she ever purchased with her allowance.

The one that her parents played in the car on road trips.

The one she always requested at weddings.

The one she sang the incorrect lyrics to until very recently.

Jack never really thought about how his music fit into the stories of other people's lives. So much of his work was an expression of his own emotions and lived experiences that he knew would resonate with others. They were his stories, but now he wondered how much of his music accompanied the creation of a memory.

Glancing over the top of his glasses, Jack watched Mia move around the room, watering plants and dusting off their large flat leaves. Despite her being at the front of the room during every class, Jack seldom saw her. He was engrossed in a moving meditation, focused only on his breath and the corresponding movement. Though the movement challenged his body, in many ways, his mind was at rest.

Movement.

Rest.

Memory.

Jack had something percolating, but he couldn't quite grasp it. He followed the delicate thread as it formed...something. He needed to write it down. Jack looked around him for a sheet of paper and any kind of writing utensil.

Nothing. Just Mia's laptop and his phone.

No, none of those would work.

"I'm so sorry, June-bug," Jack said as he slipped his legs out from under the drowsy retriever.

Once free of her weight, he sprang up and ran for the cubby where he kept his backpack. He pulled out a notebook and let the words and the melody flow from his mind to the paper through his hand. Whatever inkling of a song he had dried up as quickly as it came, and he stared at the half-filled page. It wasn't much, but it was more than he'd written in months.

Taking his notebook with him, he eased himself down into his pillow pile.

"Everything okay?" Mia asked as she turned down the music.

"Yeah. I thought I had something, but it didn't go anywhere."

"Sounds like there's a crack in the dam though," Mia said, plopping down next to him.

Mia used fragrance sparingly in the studio, but she routinely applied an oil mixture to the insides of her wrists before class. The now familiar trio of lavender, sandalwood, and peppermint tickled his nose.

"Maybe a little one," he conceded. "Let me show you the bookkeeping system I set up for you."

Mia inched closer and leaned forward, bringing her attention to the laptop between them.

Jack went over the new software and showed her how it connected with her existing calendars. Notifications and reminders would pop up well before bills were due, and prompted easy payments for things not on autopay.

"I think this system will work for you, but if it doesn't, it's pretty customizable," he said when he was finished.

"Systems tend to work for me until they don't," she replied. "But I think between this and finally getting medication for my ADHD, it will help a lot. Thank you."

Mia had once mentioned a history of anxiety and depression, but the ADHD diagnosis was new information. Having it himself, he recognized some of the symptoms in Mia, and it confirmed what he already knew.

"How long have you been without it?" Jack hadn't had any issues getting his own prescriptions filled while in Firefly Ridge, but he knew other people hadn't been as lucky.

"My whole life," she laughed. "I got diagnosed a few years ago in my mid-thirties."

Jack nodded. "The former gifted kid who fell through the cracks because you weren't bouncing off the walls like me."

"Nailed it," Mia said. "When you're a yoga teacher, it's really easy to get sucked into the worst parts of the wellness space. Which is aggravating because yoga is the opposite of all that shit. Between the really shitty health insurance plan and the pressure to avoid medication, I just never tried."

That explained the vibe shift Jack saw in Chasing Ember's social media content. Mia left a lot unsaid, but Jack could fill in the blanks. He didn't know if Mia and Ember were also romantically involved, but their business partnership and friendship had a lot of similarities to his previous marriage. The difference seemed to be that Jack and Tomas spent more time apart than together. By the time Jack realized he was being pulled into things he didn't care for, someone would leave for a tour or a movie shoot, and Jack would go back to being his authentic self.

"Well, having lived in L.A. for the last five years, I don't have any experience with toxic wellness," Jack said sarcastically. "So I can't relate."

"I didn't think so." Mia laughed. "I have an appointment next week with a new psychiatrist, and I think store-bought neurotransmitters will be a good tool in my toolkit."

"I think so, too."

Their eyes met, and he returned her smile. Her lips were glossy with a hint of red from the lip balm she always had stashed in her pocket. The dark liner and light pink brushed on her eyelids enhanced the honey-brown eyes that flitted over his face like she was also trying to read his thoughts.

What would she do if he grabbed her dimpled chin and kissed her softly?

Would she kiss him back?

Run her tongue over his?

Tangle her fingers in his hair?

Jack was in a losing battle with his self-restraint when a crack of lightning and a crash of thunder shook the building and flickered the lights. They both jumped, then laughed at their reaction, extinguishing the tension between them.

Mia

Mia trimmed another branch from the overgrown Bradford pear reaching too far into her driveway. She hated the tree and its dead-fish-scented blooms, but hiring someone to cut it down moved to the bottom of her priority list when she took over the studio.

Although, now that Jack was handling some of her administrative tasks, she could dedicate time to making that call. The new bookkeeping system he set up streamlined a lot of the work, and she offered more than once to take over, but he continued to brush her off.

"I'm making use of that music business management degree I worked so moderately hard for," he'd said before leaving the studio the day before.

Being gorgeous and creative already made Jack hard to resist, and now the guy was throwing spreadsheet competency into the mix. If he were just doing her books, Mia would have floated the idea of doing other things together—preferably naked. Though she'd settle for partially clothed.

But after his trial week was over, Jack signed up for a studio membership, taking naked adult activities off the table.

Chasing Ember had never been *that* kind of yoga studio, but Mia was making an intentional effort to change the vibe of the place to something more welcoming and inclusive. Having been the student screwing the yoga teacher several times, she knew from experience that it wasn't conducive to welcoming or inclusive vibes.

She added the branch and several others to a growing pile in the back of her property, then used the bottom of her tank top to wipe the sweat from her face and the dirty thoughts from her mind. Jack was on his way over with her laptop, and this wasn't the time to test if her new ADHD medication improved her impulse control.

Mia was taking some large gulps from her water bottle when June bolted from where she was napping under the bare branches of a poplar tree. Joining her dog behind the short wooden fence on the side of the house, they watched Jack's white SUV come up the dirt road and turn into her driveway.

Her stomach did a few flips of excitement with a hint of nerves. Despite her crush and the growing sexual tension she pretended didn't exist, the studio acted as neutral territory. There were well established professional lines and consumer expectations. Jack coming to her home started to blur those lines like a morning fog rolling over the mountains.

June pushed past Mia to squeeze through the gate, and Jack greeted the excited retriever with equal fervor. He'd been doing most of the bookkeeping after class, but for one reason or another, he asked if he could bring her computer home and offered to return it the following day.

Mia insisted it could wait. Jack insisted he return it.

"If she keeps running to me, I may end up stealing her," Jack teased as he grabbed her laptop from the backseat.

"You'd bring her back the minute she came home covered in the remains of some dead animal," Mia said.

"Does that happen often?"

"At least once a year," she replied, taking the bag from him.

Jack cringed. "Sorry, June. I won't be kidnapping you anytime soon."

Mia didn't expect Jack to stay, but she also didn't want him to leave.

"Do you want to stay for a bit? I can make some coffee."

Mia never drank coffee in the middle of the day anymore. If anything, she drank tea, but she knew Jack was a coffee guy and wasn't confident about his stance on tea. Jack's hold on her made lack of sleep worth it. Blurred lines be damned.

"Sure!" Jack exclaimed. He laughed awkwardly as he ran his fingers through his hair and rubbed the back of his neck. "I mean, I'd love coffee. Coffee would be great."

Mia led Jack around the house to the covered stone patio, June running ahead and returning to her leafy bed under the poplar tree.

"Get comfy," she instructed. "I'll be right back."

"Tea is good, too," Jack said quickly before she could leave. "I know you don't really drink coffee in the afternoon."

Mia was shocked to a standstill. She hadn't realized he was so familiar with her beverage habits, and his consideration turned her insides to pudding.

"Tea is probably a better idea this time of day," she agreed.

Needing a few minutes to compose herself, Mia declined Jack's offer to help. While the water heated in the kettle, Mia busied herself preparing a tray with mugs, some milk, sugar, and local honey. Anytime her mind wandered to dissecting Jack's attention to detail, she pulled her focus back on her task. The practice should have gotten easier considering how often she did it to get her mind off of him, but it didn't.

When she returned, Jack was slouched in one of the oversized lounge chairs that faced a collection of busy bird feeders.

"The tea just needs to steep for five-ish minutes," she said, putting the tray on a low wicker table. Mia flopped down in the lounge chair next to Jack, her body registering that she hadn't sat in hours. She held out a plastic container of chocolate chip cookies she'd made the previous night.

"How's your yard work going?" Jack asked, lazily grabbing a cookie.

"What makes you say that?"

Jack sat up and leaned over the arm of the chair, his body only inches from hers. He smiled confidently. "You have dirt stains on your leggings and your shirt. And..."

His hand skimmed her cheek. She held her breath, and her heart pounded, anticipating his touch.

"You have a few small twigs in your hair." He gently plucked something from near her temple and flicked it onto the ground. "And you told me yesterday you planned on doing some gardening."

Mia exhaled, willing her body to calm. "Right. I did say that."

She ran her fingers over her hair, finding more bits of bark and leaves. Twenty years ago, she would have been mortified. But twenty years ago, she never would have let Jack come over before she had time to shower, blow out her hair, and put on makeup.

While Mia probably looked like a hot mess, Jack just looked hot. Occasionally when Mia bumped into a student outside the studio, it took her a few moments to recognize them. But Street-Clothes Jack more closely resembled Rock-Star Jack, and Mia found herself a little starstruck.

And a little aroused.

His hair had gotten long enough that he pulled the top half into a small ponytail in class. But now it flopped lazily to one side, his loose curls tamed by some kind of product. He'd trimmed his beard and cleaned up the soft bristles on his throat. His glasses hung from the V made by the open buttons of his deep brown Henley. A bit of the hem was tucked into soft dark-wash jeans over thick-soled boots. The leather band of a silver watch was wrapped around one wrist, and silver rings adorned most of his fingers. A fresh coat of dark blue polish replaced the chipped black he wore last.

"This is a really nice yard." Jack sat back in his chair. "What were you working on?"

"I was transplanting a few fall plants that didn't seem happy where they were and trimming back a few trees."

Mia explained how the previous owners used the property as a vacation rental and clear-cut most of the yard to keep maintenance costs down. "You don't have to pay a landscaper to bag leaves and trim bushes if you don't have any trees or bushes."

She added a few native plants every season in a slow, but sustainable, effort to bring back some of the flora that once thrived there.

"I miss spending my free time out here. I don't think I realized the benefits until recently," she said, unable to hide the sadness in her voice. "It was easier when I had a business partner, and I split my studio time with her. Now I'm not home as much, and when I am, it's late or I'm exhausted."

"The business part of running a business definitely takes a lot more time than I ever realized." Jack slid off his chair and poured two cups of tea. "Some people like it, but I never did."

"So why did you offer to help me with mine?" Mia waved off his offers of milk and sweetener and took the mug from him.

Jack sank down into the chair, a teasing smile on his face, but he focused his gaze on his mug. "That's not how I remember it. You offered it as a project, and I accepted."

"Fuck off." Mia laughed and nudged his leg with her bare foot just enough that his tea sloshed a bit, threatening to tip over the rim. Jack laughed harder trying to recover without spilling the hot beverage on himself.

"And my therapist says I try to fix other people's problems to avoid dealing with my own."

Mia nodded knowingly. "Your problems being your lack of creative mojo?"

Jack nodded, then touched the mug to his lips.

"How's that going?"

Jack sighed. "Better, but I'm still really far off from a complete album. I haven't wanted to throw my guitar off the swinging bridge in a few weeks, so that's progress."

Mia laughed at the relatability and raised her mug in salute. Jack tapped it with his own, and they took another sip. They sat in relaxed silence, watching birds come and go from the feeders.

"Sometimes, I think we get stuck so we're forced to change," Mia pondered out loud. "I've been thinking about change a lot since Ember left. I was a different person when we opened the studio together. About a year ago, I started feeling trapped in an environment that I created but no longer believed in."

"So you changed?" Jack asked.

"No." Mia laughed, realizing her example didn't really fit her theory. "But kinda. When I became the sole owner of the studio, I could keep everything the same or I could make the studio a reflection of how I've changed. I guess the petty part of me wanted to do all the things Ember vetoed."

"Spite is a powerful motivator," Jack agreed with a laugh. "Why keep the name?"

It was a simple answer, but Mia took a beat to sip her tea and gather her thoughts. "Name recognition. And to ease members into the changes. I also have a closet full of branded merchandise that I can't afford to replace at the moment."

"Fair enough." Jack nodded and sipped his tea. "Why Chasing Ember Yoga Studio?"

"It's just a play on our names." Mia shrugged. "Mia Chase. Ember Ross. Chasing Ember."

"That's it?" Jack said in disbelief. "No profound meaning? Just your names?"

"Just our names," Mia assured. "My therapist suggested it was a metaphor for our relationship...or friendship or whatever.

But at the time, we really just liked the sound of it. It sounds pretty deep, right?"

"It does." Jack tilted his head back and laughed like he was just let in on the most obvious of secrets.

"Not as deep as Concrete Tears, though," Mia teased.

"Fuck off." Jack returned Mia's earlier nudge with his own.

"I love teaching. And I really love the community. But I really fucking hate running a business."

"A business or *this* business?" Jack pressed.

"Fuck if I know," Mia scoffed.

Now it was Jack's turn to laugh and raise his mug. "Maybe it's time for a change."

Mia returned his salute, his words echoing in her ears.

Maybe he's right.

Jack

"Inhale, two, three, four. Hold, two, three, four."

Jack followed Mia's soothing guidance through a breathing exercise, but no matter how hard he tried, her voice failed to hold his focus.

"Exhale, two, three, four. Hold, two, three, four."

It was unusual, for sure. Her voice had been commanding his attention since the day they met. Whether she was hollering for her dog or reciting a guided meditation, his ears tuned out everything else but her.

He still had trouble with these quiet moments in stillness. His brain wasn't wired for it, and he'd been learning to cut himself a little slack. Once they got moving, his mind usually settled.

But not today.

Jack's mind wandered, turning over fragments of verses and melodies that he struggled to connect. His body moved through the familiar motions of Mia's sequence, but his mind wasn't there. He floated through the postures on muscle memory alone.

Before joining the rest of the class in tree pose, he downed half the ice-cold liquid in his water bottle, hoping it would wash away the gunk taking up too much space in his head.

Jack planted his right foot and lifted his left to the inside of his calf. His body shook, and he put his arms out to recover his balance, but he couldn't save it. Frustrated, he started over.

"Remember," Mia said to the class. Or maybe it was just for him. "Pine trees sway in the wind so they don't break."

Jack's foot hit the floor with a thud.

"That's it," he whispered.

He had it.

"I have to go." Jack rushed to clean up his space. "I'm sorry."

Everyone stopped their own practice to watch him. "Nothing's wrong. I just need to go. Right now."

Mia looked confused, concerned. Hurt. Students occasionally left in the middle of class, but never so abruptly. He would explain it all to her, just not right now.

Jack was tempted to ignore whoever was ringing his doorbell, but it was nine at night, and it wouldn't be the first time in the last few days he forgot he had placed a food delivery order. He stumbled to the door, fighting a cramp in his leg from sitting on the floor for hours.

Instead of pizza, he opened the door to find something more tantalizing than his dessert.

"Hey," Mia said with a sheepish smile.

Her faded purple hair was twisted into a long braid that fell over one shoulder, and a rainbow knit headband covered her ears from the biting cold. She wore thick joggers and a heavy fleece jacket. Comfortable loungewear compared to the styled athletic gear he normally saw her in. Like he imagined she'd look on a weekend curled up on the couch with a book or her favorite movie.

"I'm so sorry for just showing up. And for using several questionable research techniques to find your address, but it's been two days, and you weren't picking up your phone. I started to worry and then I got anxious, and I started thinking all these crazy things like maybe you died..."

Jack didn't let her finish. He took a step forward and cupped Mia's cold-kissed cheeks in both hands. The cadence of her breath was the metronome for a symphony he'd been yearning to play. Her honey-brown eyes looked at him with the same longing.

"I'm very much alive," he whispered.

The ravenous need to kiss her overwhelmed him.

The pattern suddenly became very clear. He'd hit an endless well of inspiration and poured it into his music. To keep from drowning in the overflow, he pointed it at his muse. Much of his best work was written on the ashes of these passionate highs with Tomas. Their passion burned hot but quick, leaving Jack depleted with nothing left to give to their marriage.

He had to break the pattern.

He dropped his hands from her face and pulled her into his chest, inhaling the comforting notes of peppermint and sandalwood.

"I've been writing," he said, holding her tightly. "The dam broke, and I had to follow the current. I'm sorry I bolted from class, and I'm sorry I worried you."

"That's so great!" Mia's voice was muffled, but her excitement sounded genuine. "I'm thrilled for you."

Jack let go and wrapped his arms around his chest to keep from pulling her back into his embrace.

Into his cabin.

Into his bed.

"I'll stop distracting you then," she said, stuffing her hands into her pockets. "Just send me proof of life every couple of days, okay?"

"I will. I'm sorry."

Mia hesitated. The disappointment showed on her face and in the rounding of her shoulders.

Jack hated himself at the moment and considered giving in to his selfish impulses.

But Mia was right. It was time for a change.

Mia

Mia stepped into the cold mountain air, the chill on her bare skin a relief from the warmth inside her studio. She always turned up the heat for restorative classes during the winter, but her aversion to a hot room worsened after turning forty.

Mia propped open the back door and popped the trunk of her SUV. She made three trips from the building, filling the vehicle with overflowing baskets of dirty towels and woven blankets. All the studio linens would get a run through an industrial washer during the studio's holiday break, and

Mia's gift to herself was paying someone else to do it this year. Before locking everything up, she grabbed a small overnight bag from her backseat.

It was the night of the charity concert at Trixy's Tavern, and Mia had a hunch she'd feel sweaty and gross after class. Ember never gave Mia a straight answer as to why they had a full bathroom with a shower but no washer and dryer. Mia wasn't mad about it on nights like this.

While the water warmed, Mia organized her things and sent Jack a text.

MIA: In case I don't get to talk to you before the show starts, break a leg!

MIA: Or is that just a theater thing? Should I not say that?

Between holing up in his cabin writing music

and Thanksgiving, Mia hadn't seen Jack in weeks. True to his word, however, he did send her proof of life updates every couple of days. The exchanges were quick, and while they eased Mia's anxiety about his health and well-being, his absence from her professional and personal life only made her fall harder.

JACK: I think it's mostly a theater thing. But I've done Broadway and shit so I'll allow it ;)

Mia giggled at Jack's reply.
Broadway and shit.

JACK: Thanks for thinking about me.

Mia considered replying that she was always thinking about him. She thought about him when a bill got paid on time and when their shared favorite songs played on the radio. She thought about him when Juniper took off running after a squirrel and when she wore her fleece jacket that still had whispers of his scent. She thought about him late at night when she was too wound up to go to sleep.

Mia couldn't stop thinking about him.

She decided against saying anything. She wasn't sure how he'd receive a response like that, and she didn't want to throw him off before a show.

Considering his credit card was just charged to renew his membership for another month, there was still the whole business ethics thing.

Instead, she replied with a smiley face and took her thoughts of Jack into the shower.

Mia lucked into a parking spot across the street and whispered a thank you to all deities known and unknown that she wouldn't have to walk from the public lot in her heeled booties. She couldn't afford a trip to urgent care after twisting an ankle running to the bar from up the block.

She'd mostly given up on heels, and the ones she held onto were reasonably comfortable. But it'd been months (years?) since she had gotten this dolled up, and she underestimated how long it would take her to get ready. She also didn't know if the bar would be hot or cold, so she dressed for both. Covered only by lacy tights and a ruffled miniskirt, the sharp cold hit Mia's legs the moment she opened the car door. A cozy sweater balanced out the outfit. It was too thick to wear comfortably with a jacket, but her proximity to the bar meant she could leave the extra layer behind.

Every small town had a Trixy's Tavern. A bar that never changed, even when the owners did. Sheila wasn't Trixy's original owner, but no one was quite sure how it came into her possession. As usual, the theories were probably more fun than the truth.

Murder, blackmail, gambling. Maybe all three. Sheila refused to tell.

North Carolina banned smoking inside bars almost fifteen years earlier, but the tobacco from cigarettes past still hung in the air, etched permanently into the wooden rafters. Mia found a patch of space against the wall and scanned the room. Patrons filled every booth and every table, and even more stood in a crowd in front of the stage.

Jackson Hunter sold out arenas that held over fifteen thousand people. Tonight, he and other local musicians would play for a crowd of about 200. Sheila got on stage, and Mia took advantage of the audience surging forward to grab an open spot at the bar.

Despite Jack's notoriety, he wasn't headlining the show. That spot went to the New River Boys, the local bluegrass band that was arguably more well-known across the Southeast than Jackson Hunter. Jack was up third, giving Mia a chance to order a drink and chat with some other small business owners in attendance.

A tall blond in scrub pants and a polo shirt waved Mia over to an open spot near one corner of the stage. Physical therapist Ashton Medlin and Mia had a casual arrangement in which Mia referred her students to Ashton for PT and Ashton sent their clients to Mia for yoga.

"Did you see my email with the open studio times?" Mia asked after greeting her friend.

Ashton nodded while taking a sip of their beer.

"I saw you sent it, but I haven't read it yet. I came straight from work." Ashton gestured to their outfit. Ashton was ready to open their own practice and approached Mia about renting the yoga studio space when it wasn't being used for classes.

The blues band on stage finished their set to thunderous applause. Mia saw Jack waiting in the proverbial wings with Sheila.

Ashton must have seen him too. "I heard Jackson Hunter takes classes at Chasing Ember."

Mia replied with a shrug. "Come to class and find out."

Sheila got behind the microphone, and the audience quieted.

"My servers tell me that Jackson Hunter is some kind of famous musician these days, but if you've been comin' here awhile, you'll probably remember him better as the sweet-faced lead singer of that band with Charlie Murphy's boy."

The name elicited gasps of surprise and murmurs of recognition from locals over forty. Jack crossed the stage to cheers and applause.

He placed a notebook on the barstool next to the microphone. Somehow, despite the blinding lights and sea of faces, Jack found her, and their eyes locked. That familiar devilish smile appeared with a smoldering gaze that twisted Mia's belly into knots.

Seeing Jack on stage was a stark reminder that he was, in fact, a legitimate rock star. He introduced himself and made a few jokes, but Mia didn't hear any of it. She was too distracted by the way his dark gray dress shirt was tucked loosely into the waist of his black leather pants. The top few buttons were undone, exposing the collar of a white top underneath and bold sections of his chest tattoos. One arm hung lazily over his vintage Gibson guitar while the other lightly held the microphone stand. The incandescent lights glinted off the silver chains around his neck and the rings on his fingers. Mia saw his mostly bare arms several times a week, and they were a joy to look at. But by some mystery of the universe, they were even more sexy when his sleeves were rolled to just below the elbow. Between the explicit display of his tattooed forearms and the slutty glasses he slipped on before addressing the crowd, Mia was wound more tightly than one of Jack's guitar strings.

"I grew up in Durham, but my friends and I spent so much time here it's like y'all raised me," Jack said, his gaze leaving Mia's to look around the room. "That's why coming back to Firefly Ridge to reconnect with my music felt like coming home."

The crowd roared, but in the heartbeat of a moment before Jack started playing, the room was empty and silent, and Mia knew this set was just for her.

In what he called an ode to his musical journey, Jack began his three-song set with a cover of Green Day's "When I Come Around". It was one he and his buddies performed regularly at Trixy's before they were old enough to drink and understood things like performance licensing. It also happened to be one of Mia's favorites from the *Dookie* album.

The second, from Jack's most recent album, was a popular track that was used as background sound for over a million video edits across three social media platforms. A few people around Mia said some variation of, "Oh! I know this song!"

The third was new. Composed in the few weeks he sequestered himself in his cabin. Jack's eyes found hers again, and there was no mistaking who he was speaking to. "I wrote this here in Firefly Ridge, and it's still a work in progress," he said. "And a little bit of a different sound, but I hope y'all enjoy it."

It was a different sound. A little more bluesy and a little more twangy. Like it was coated in the hazy blue mist that gave this section of the Appalachians its name.

Mia didn't know much about music. She didn't play an instrument, and her singing abilities were passable for karaoke and road trips. But music, especially performed live, was an art that she felt deep in the hollows of her bones.

And it was the feeling of Jack's music that struck Mia as something new. It was deeper and more soulful. Passionate and honest. Sensual and seductive. Paired with Jack's spellbinding gaze that seldom left hers, the emotions enveloped her, giving her goosebumps and forming a lump in her chest. She wasn't sad, but she wanted to cry, or cry out, she couldn't tell.

The song was over, but the sensations lingered as the thunderous applause shook dust from the tobacco-stained rafters. It was only when Jack left the stage that Mia noticed her phone vibrating in her pocket.

She had multiple missed calls and texts from her alarm company. The security alarm at the studio had been triggered, and they were checking in.

After saying goodbye to Ashton, Mia used her voice assistant to compose a text to Jack as she made her way through the crowd and out the door to her car.

MIA: That was AMAZING!! I had to run. Studio emergency. I'll text you later. Have fun tonight!

Mia threw her phone in her bag, opting to call the alarm company once she got to her building. She didn't need to, though, because when she arrived, she was met with the strobing red lights of a police car.

"Fan-fucking-tastic."

Jack

After responding to Mia's text, Jack checked his phone every thirty seconds for the next fifteen minutes. Then he called, but after five rings it went to voicemail.

He tried to convince himself everything was fine, but he wouldn't believe it until he heard or saw Mia for himself. Jack told Sheila he was leaving to check on Mia, and she dismissed him with an irritating—but endearing—smile.

JACK: I'm heading to the studio.

Jack pulled up to the studio, finding the building dark and quiet like every other storefront on the block. Mia's car was also missing. His chest tightened with panic as he pulled up Mia's home address in the GPS before texting her again.

JACK: Proof of life goes both ways, ya know. Heading to your place.

Jack sighed a breath of relief when he saw lights on inside Mia's house and her car in the driveway. A text came through just as he was throwing his car in park.

MIA: Sorry! I have a good excuse though. Side door is open. Come on in.

Jack's heart rate started to settle, and

he could breathe a little easier. Juniper greeted him in the mudroom with subdued excitement appropriate for the late hour.

Jack found Mia at the kitchen island with a dirty white kitten eating canned tuna from a small plate.

"Studio emergency?" He arched a brow, pulling out one of the barstools tucked under the island.

Mia sighed a laugh and added another forkful of tuna to the plate. "At the end of your set, I saw a thousand missed calls from my security company because the alarm had been triggered. All the doors were still locked and none of the windows messed with.

"I had the door propped open earlier and this little monster must have snuck in when I was loading my car. She went exploring after I left, knocked some plants off the bookshelf, and set off the alarm. I found her hiding in the bathroom after I was allowed inside."

"Well, at least she waited long enough for you to catch the whole set," he said, scratching the small space between the kitten's ears. She was caked in dirt and couldn't have been older than a couple of months.

"So what's next?" he asked.

"I'm selling the studio."

Jack froze, his eyes going wide and his mouth gaping. "I was talking about the cat but go on."

"Oh, Stella Regina Chase? I have a cat now, obviously. She's literally in my house. What else is there to say about it?"

"Yeah, I guess you're right." Jack prompted Mia to continue.

"My friend Ashton is a PT looking to open their own practice, so they reached out about renting the space when I wasn't using it. And from those conversations, I started toying with the idea of closing Chasing Ember and selling them the building."

When the plate was empty, Mia picked up the kitten—Stella—and cradled it against her chest. Mia tilted her head, signaling for Jack to follow her into the living room.

The last time he was at Mia's place, they'd spent the whole day outside, only coming in to use the bathroom or grab some snacks. Jack sat on the couch nearby. It was well-loved, with mismatched throw pillows and a sprinkling of dog fur.

"Getting pulled away from Trixy's tonight made up my mind," Mia said as she placed Stella into a shallow box on top of a heating pad and some soft towels. "This isn't how I want to teach anymore."

"How do you want to teach?"

"I'm going to enclose my patio and turn it into a studio space," she said. "Smaller classes, private sessions, less overhead. And if it doesn't work out, I still have an enclosed patio and my job at the college."

"Are you sure?" he asked, but he already knew the answer.

She nodded and stood in front of him. In a regular chair, their height difference wouldn't have seemed so dramatic. But sitting on the low couch, Mia towered over him, even without shoes on.

"When you helped me with my bookkeeping, I finally had time to think," she said, inching closer. Jack parted his knees, encouraging her to step between his legs.

"You eased a burden and gave me the chance to breathe and time to reflect on what I really wanted." Mia's slow, breathy voice matched the lust in her darkened eyes.

Jack slid his hands over his thighs and hesitated a beat before resting his fingers just above her knees. She hadn't changed since getting home, and he cursed the delicate fabric of her lacy tights for denying him the touch of her bare skin. She stepped closer, and the space between them shrank faster than Jack's self-control.

"And I want to do things a little differently," she said.

His hands moved up her legs, over the ruffles of her miniskirt. "Well, I guess I'll have to transfer my membership to your new location for private sessions."

"Sorry. No transfers," she said. Cupping the back of his neck, she climbed onto his lap; straddling his hips, her skirt hiked up her thighs.

He held her steady, his fingers pressed into her legs, longing to feel the curves of her body. Mia leaned forward, her lips fluttering in the crook of his neck. His hardened dick screamed for release, and Jack took a slow breath, relishing the anticipation.

"Because," she whispered, her breath hot against his skin, "the things I want to do with you right now get really complicated when money is involved. I hope you're okay with that policy change."

Jack turned his head until his lips brushed against hers. "I love change."

The words were barely out of his mouth when Mia pressed her lips to his and a blissful moan escaped with her exhale. Mia relaxed into his touch and parted her lips to welcome a sweep of his tongue.

With a little nip on her bottom lip, Jack pulled away from her mouth and trailed his tongue down her throat to lavish kisses in the curve of her shoulder. Mia undid each button of his collared shirt in quick succession, stripping it off his shoulders and down his arms until he was forced to relinquish his grasp on her body. Jack took off his tank top and let it drop somewhere beside him.

At the same time, Mia untucked her sweater and pulled it over her head, taking her bra with it. Jack explored her perfect breasts with his tongue and dug his fingers into her ass. Mia writhed on his lap, grinding against his dick that strained behind the zipper of his pants.

Mia slowly broke their connection with light kisses over his neck and pulled away when he tried to do the same.

"You ripped my favorite tights," Mia said, her tone seductive and scolding.

In his fervor, Jack hadn't realized he'd torn finger-sized holes in the lace. She slid off his lap and once again stood between his knees. Her cheeks glistened, and her lipstick was slightly smudged.

"Take them off," she demanded. "Gently."

"Yes, ma'am." Jack had long given up the Southern honorific he was raised with, and this wasn't at all the situation in which he expected it to resurface.

Jack slid his hands under the waistband, catching the elastic with the web of his thumbs. His hands sank down Mia's thick legs, pushing the tights to her ankles so she could step out of them. Her skirt was the only clothing that remained, and it made him absolutely feral. His hands retreated up her calves, thankful that the offending fabric was finally gone.

But Mia put her hands on his forearms, stopping him halfway up her thighs.

"Not yet." She dragged her teeth over her bottom lip. "Take off your pants."

"Yes, ma'am." Jack bent over to untie his boots.

"Good boy," she praised, twirling a lock of his hair around her finger.

When his shoes were gone, he sat up, then stood. Mia watched him hungrily, licking her lips. Jack followed her tongue with the thumb of his right hand while his left hand undid his belt, button, and fly.

"Impressive skills," Mia said as she helped him ease his leather pants and his boxers down his legs. If he hadn't been enjoying the anticipation so much, he would have regretted wearing pants so cumbersome to remove.

Jack grabbed her ass and pulled her into him. "Doing impressive things with my hands is kind of my job." He smiled.

To prove his point, he spun her around, pressing his chest against her back. He bathed in the heat of her body and the scent of her skin. He slipped one arm under hers to palm her breast. Mia leaned into him, throwing her arm behind his head as best as her reach would allow. His free hand slid over the hills of her stomach, under the elastic of her skirt, and slowed to an agonizing pace towards her clit. He dragged a finger between her wet labia. Mia cried out, thrusting her hips forward. Then he did it over and over again while he rolled her hardened nipple with his fingertips.

Jack followed the sounds of her building pleasure like they were a roadmap to heaven. Every sigh, every cry, catalogued in his mind. Every move of her quivering body that brought her closer to bliss imprinted in his muscle memory.

Jack was familiar with Mia's natural breathing. Breathwork was done in every class, and he started to notice the slight changes in Mia's breath when they were together. The quick, shallow inhales and exhales were completely new and music to his ears. The faster her breath, the harder her heart pounded against the hand on her chest.

Squeezing one breast in a tight grip, he used the same pressure to rub her clit.

Mia moaned a curse, then sighed his name as her body trembled. Her head tipped back, and she held her breath, releasing it with a laugh.

"What other job skills are useful in the bedroom?"

Jack heard the playfulness in her raspy voice, and he spun her around before she could go limp. Her cherry-red cheeks glistened with sweat and smudged mascara coated her lower lid. Her right breast was pink from his manhandling.

Jack sat down and lifted her skirt, pulling her closer by her hips. "I figured this one would be obvious."

Still swollen from his fingers, he ran the tip of his tongue between her labia. Her legs buckled, but Jack held her hips steady as he devoured her. Mia's fingers combed through his hair, guiding him with subtle changes.

Goosebumps erupted over her skin, and her long, slow breaths became short and quick.

"Don't make me come yet," Mia hissed through her teeth.

Jack slowed, and Mia's breathing slowed with him.

"I have an IUD," she whimpered. "I haven't had sex since my last negative test."

Jack licked her with the flat of his tongue like she was his favorite flavor.

"Vasectomy," he said without pulling away. He licked her again. "Same."

He licked her twice more before she gripped his hair and tilted his head back. "Good, because I want you deep inside me."

"Yes, ma'am."

"I'll be right back." Mia kissed him before walking swiftly from the living room, her skirt bouncing with the movement and flashing her ass.

Mia

Mia ran past June and Stella, silently thanking them for staying in their beds and not making things weird like pets tended to do.

She pulled a small bottle of water-based lube from her nightstand. Her aging body was changing in ways no one warned her about, and she wouldn't let it ruin her good time.

Jack was right where Mia left him on the couch. Waiting, but not patiently. She could see his body vibrating with need.

"Don't be stingy with it."

She handed him the bottle and made quick work of opening it while she kneeled over him. She gripped the back of the couch to hold herself steady. Ever the multitasker, Jack sucked on her tits as he squeezed a generous amount of lube on the head of his cock and worked it down his shaft.

Mia pulled back to look him in the eyes. His pupils were large pools of black pushing out the vivid green in his hazel eyes. "You have to enter slowly."

Jack cupped her cheek with his dry hand. "Whatever you want and whatever you need."

Then he kissed her like she was the air he breathed. It was passionate and desperate, triggering the same emotions in her as his music.

She hovered over him, the tip grazing her sensitive skin. The anticipation fueled the desperation in his kiss. Unsure of the sensation she'd be met with, she exhaled slowly as she slid down his shaft. He filled her, and she sighed with pleasurable discomfort.

She found the right depth, and Jack met every roll of her hips with a thrust that reverberated through her body. Every pulse rocked her like the chorus of her favorite song.

Mia was fixated on the feel of Jack's skin against hers. The dusting of hair on his chest that tickled her nose. The salty metallic taste of his nipple rings on her tongue. Guttural moans vibrated in his throat against her lips. She couldn't remember the last time she'd felt so attuned to her body as it connected with someone else's.

Jack slowed their rhythm. "May I make you come now?"

"Fuck. Yes, you may."

In a swift move Mia didn't realize she was still capable of, Jack had her flipped onto her back, propped perfectly against her mismatched throw pillows, save for the one Jack was kneeling on. He squeezed more lube onto his dick and stroked himself slick.

Following her lead, Jack pressed inside her. Slow and deep. He shifted a bit here. Adjusted a bit there. Stopping only when he found a position that made Mia beg for more. Jack found his rhythm. The perfect tempo to bring her to the edge. She reached between her legs, ready to take herself over, but Jack got there first, pressing his thumb exactly where she wanted it.

Needed it.

Mia's body flooded with a river of euphoria. Her hips lifted, taking Jack deeper and sending another wave of sweet relief and bliss. Digging his fingers into her flesh, Jack's body shook with his release. He eased out of her carefully and collapsed between Mia's knees, his head resting on her thigh. She curled his hair around her fingers as they lingered there in silence, their slowing breaths the only sound.

Until a tiny cat climbed up the side of the couch with a shrill meow and made it weird.

Mia

Mia opened the back door, letting June run out first before stepping onto the patio. Her heavy fleece robe and hot coffee were minimally effective at keeping her warm against the winter mountain air. It was the winter solstice, and it smelled like snow and a wood-burning stove. Swooping birds were dark spots against the lavender morning sky. For the first time in a long time, she felt at peace with herself and the journey in front of her.

The man she left dozing in her bed was the only bit of uncertainty. Mia wanted to share this next chapter with him. But with his albums written and his contracts fulfilled, he had no reason to stay in Firefly Ridge.

When the chill was no longer refreshing, she called June inside. She heard Jack's hoarse voice coming from the bedroom. It sounded like one side of a phone conversation, but Mia couldn't make out what he was saying. She was tempted to snoop, but instead, she took her time preparing him a cup of coffee to give him some privacy.

When he was done, she carried his coffee in one hand and Stella in the other.

"Who calls so early on a Saturday so close to Christmas?" Mia asked, handing him the mug and putting Stella on her lap. June was already dozing at the foot of the bed.

Jack set his phone down on the nightstand. "My lawyer. She's overnighting a few contracts."

"Ooh anything good? A movie deal maybe?"

Jack laughed and took a sip of his coffee. "No movie deals. But I am buying a house."

Mia had trouble rationalizing the mischievous look in his eye with the disappointment in the pit of her stomach. "Oh. Yeah? Where?"

"Here," he said, then sipped his coffee.

"Here? Like in North Carolina?"

Jack laughed again and put his coffee on the nightstand. "No, Firefly Ridge. I'm buying Richie's family's cabin. The one I've been living in for the past six months."

Jack turned towards her and pulled her close. "I came back here because I thought there was magic in that house. But the magic wasn't in the house. It's in this place. The air. The animals. The people." He kissed the tip of her nose.

"But if I'm going to stay, I need a place to live. And Richie's parents have been talking about selling it for years."

He kissed her softly, and her stomach fluttered, the last bit of uncertainty dissolving like blue mountain mist.

Afterword

I hope you enjoyed reading *Chasing Ember* as much as I did writing it.

When I wrote the short story for the charity anthology I was in a season of deep depression and anxiety. To make the writing process as easy as possible, I pulled a lot from my own life or from things I was already familiar with. I didn't have the emotional or creative energy to go on deep dives into researching something obscure.

So what did I pull from real life?

My yoga-teaching philosophy

I have absolutely zero desire to open a yoga studio, but like Mia Chase, I am a yoga instructor. And my teaching philosophy is also Mia's teaching philosophy.

The questions Mia asks Jack before class are the same I ask new students (without the flirting and awkwardness. Yet, anyway).

I also have a no (bad) pain policy in my classes. I'm of the belief that yoga should feel good in your body. But more importantly, as I tell my students on the first day of class, I am not a medical professional and I write romance novels for a living so don't hurt yourself.

Mia's dog is my dog

If one of my protagonists has a dog, they're based on my dog Bailey. Maybe not in personality, but always in looks. Juniper Kimberly Chase is no exception.

We visited the Blue Ridge Mountains a few times a year back when Bailey was our only child. That dog was meant for mountain life and she handled some really challenging hikes like a champ.

Jack's mountain cabin is loosely based on a true story

To get over his writer's block, Jack sequesters himself in the same cabin he and his friends visited in their youth.

My husband and I met in our mid-20s and at that time he played keyboard in a bluegrass band made up of a bunch of friends from high school. The New River Boys is a play on their name, which I'm redacting to protect the innocent.

Instead of the Blue Ridge Mountains they went to New York's Catskill Mountains. Same mountain chain, different pronunciation (*Appa-lay-shen* vs *Appa-latch-un*), same getting stoned and writing music.

Sadly that album never got released and my husband isn't a famous musician. He does do the dishes and the laundry so he's a rock star in that sense.

Resources

While the organization Trixy's is fundraising for doesn't exist outside the Monti Novella Universe, there are several western North Carolina based organizations that are still doing important work in the area.

Asheville Dream Center

BeLoved Asheville

Hearts with Hands

Mana Food Bank

Second Harvest Food Bank

WNC Nature Center

Visit ariellamonti.com/resources for direct links

Thank yous

Thank you for choosing to read Chasing Ember. There are so many books and so little time and I'm forever grateful when a reader spends that precious time with something I wrote.

Thank you to the awesome and compassionate souls that make up NC Indies who made the original Chasing Ember happen.

To my beta readers and critique partners (the MILFs) who lent their critical eyes and thoughtful and often hilarious takes to make this book what it became.

Thank you to my physical therapist for sharing her knowledge and helping me normalize conversations about pelvic health.

I'm grateful for the work of art that Shay of Disturbed Valkyrie Design created for the cover of this book and without my copyeditor Jenny Sliger this book would be way less readable.

To my parents for their unwavering support and their belief in this endeavor.

And usually last but never least, my husband and son for the way you love me. For telling every stranger your mom is an author and believing I'm way more famous than I actually am.

About the author

Ariella is a former journalist, but uses "former" loosely. Her curiosity for all things is insatiable and research is her favorite part of any project.

She writes cozy contemporary and high stakes fantasy romances. Her work is swoony and open door absolutely not intended for readers who are under 18.

Someone once told her to write what you know so all her millennial protagonists are bisexual, neurodivergent, and live with chronic mental illness. They mostly have their life together and Ariella chronicles their coming-of-middle-age stories.

When she's not writing, she teaches yoga and falls behind on laundry. She lives in the suburbs of Raleigh, North Carolina with her husband, child, a collection of aging pets, and a flock of chickens that won't stop tearing up the new plants in her flower garden.

Read them all

Contemporary Romance

Let it Rain

Radio Romance

Chasing Ember

Fantasy Romance

Roots in Ink, Scions of Belhaven, Book 1

Bound by Ink, Scions of Belhaven Novella (Jan 2026)

SWEET MAGNOLIA SHOP

signed paperbacks
special editions
ebooks you own

ariellamonti.com/shop

www.ingramcontent.com/pod-product-compliance
Lightning Source LLC
Chambersburg PA
CBHW050415110726
47899CB00008B/2722